Copyright © 1992 Colin Robinson
First published 1992 by Blackie and Son Ltd

A CIP catalogue record for this book is
available from the British Library.

ISBN 0 216 93079 0

Blackie and Son Ltd
7 Leicester Place
London WC2H 7BP

First American edition published in 1992 by
Peter Bedrick Books
2112 Broadway
New York, NY 10023

Library of Congress Cataloging-in-Publication
Data is available for this title.

ISBN 0 87226 468 8

Printed in Singapore by Times Publishing Group

Colin Robinson

Blackie
London

Bedrick/Blackie
New York